To Maria —
It was such a beautiful
thing — to discover friendship,
to ride together,
to watch you blossom
at The Montrose
Conference.
God bless you, dear friend,
as you write in Him.

Carol Hedden
7-30-98
♥

The Christmas Crib that Zack Built

Carol S. Wedeven

illustrated by
Nell F. Fisher

Abingdon Press

Nashville

For Vern,
my creative encourager

The Christmas Crib That Zack Built

Text Copyright © 1989 by Carol Wedeven

Illustrations Copyright © 1989 by Abingdon Press

Library of Congress Cataloging-in-Publication Data

WEDEVEN, CAROL, 1942–
    The Christmas Crib that Zack built/Carol
Wedeven; illustrated by Nell Fisher.
    p.   cm.
    Summary: Relates the birth of Jesus Christ
using the pattern of the traditional cumulative
verse "This Is the House That Jack Built."
        ISBN 0-687-07816-4

    1. Jesus Christ—Nativity—Juvenile literature.
2. Crèches (Nativity scenes)—Juvenile literature.
[1. Jesus Christ-Nativity.] I. Fisher, Nell, 1938–
ill. II. Title.
BT315.2.W37   1989
232.9'2—dc19   89-263
                                                    CIP
                                                    AC

This book is printed on acid-free paper.

Manufactured in Hong Kong

This is the crib that Zack built.

This is the babe
That lay in the crib that Zack built.

This is the maid
That bore the babe
That lay in the crib that Zack built.

This is the beast
That carried the maid
That bore the babe
That lay in the crib that Zack built.

This is the hill
That tired the beast
That carried the maid
That bore the babe
That lay in the crib that Zack built.

This is the flock mid thistles that cling,
That covered the hill
That tired the beast
That carried the maid
That bore the babe
That lay in the crib that Zack built.

This is the lad with flute and sling,
That watched the flock mid thistles that cling,
That covered the hill
That tired the beast
That carried the maid
That bore the babe
That lay in the crib that Zack built.

This is the choir God sent to sing,
That scared the lad with flute and sling,
That watched the flock mid thistles that cling,
That covered the hill
That tired the beast
That carried the maid
That bore the babe
That lay in the crib that Zack built.

This is the star with rays for a ring,
That shone on the choir God sent to sing,
That scared the lad with flute and sling,
That watched the flock mid thistles that cling,
That covered the hill
That tired the beast
That carried the maid
That bore the babe
That lay in the crib that Zack built.

These are the kings with three gifts to bring,
That followed the star with rays for a ring,
That shone on the choir God sent to sing,
That scared the lad with flute and sling,
That watched the flock mid thistles that cling,
That covered the hill
That tired the beast
That carried the maid
That bore the babe
That lay in the crib that Zack built.